Escapades of Romance

Akisss Mora

Ukiyoto Publishing

All global publishing rights are held by

Ukiyoto Publishing

Published in 2023

Content Copyright © Akisss Mora
ISBN 9789360168193

All rights reserved.
No part of this publication may be reproduced, transmitted, or stored in a retrieval system, in any form by any means, electronic, mechanical, photocopying, recording or otherwise, without the prior permission of the publisher.

The moral rights of the author have been asserted.

This is a work of fiction. Names, characters, businesses, places, events, locales, and incidents are either the products of the author's imagination or used in a fictitious manner. Any resemblance to actual persons, living or dead, or actual events is purely coincidental.

This book is sold subject to the condition that it shall not by way of trade or otherwise, be lent, resold, hired out or otherwise circulated, without the publisher's prior consent, in any form of binding or cover other than that in which it is published.

www.ukiyoto.com

To my boyfriend

Contents

Chapter 1	1
Chapter 2	6
Chapter 3	11
Chapter 4	16
Chapter 5	20
Chapter 5	22
Chapter 6	25
Chapter 7	32
Chapter 8	40
Chapter 9	46
Chapter 10	49
About the Author	*51*

Chapter 1

Blood was all over the carpet, my living space was a disaster, all of my belongings had been flung all over the floor, I was a mess, as well as there was shattered glass all over the place. It felt like silk flowing into my skin with a soft grace. I am sick of being around these toxic individuals, so here I am again, destroying stuff and hurling them across the floor!

Mom inviting a guy here frightened me to death because every person she invites over to this house is a monster and they were all monsters. This room, the trauma, and that guy.

Mom's voice rang out, "Paris!" I opened my window so she wouldn't see me being so messy and out of control.

I glanced back at my room before responding to her call of "Paris!" by running for the window.

Before leaving, I apologised and asked myself why I was leaving. Is it because the man inside the house scared me? It wasn't him; he wasn't the one who had previously harmed me, scared me away, or convinced me that all men are monsters. So why am I fleeing? Damn.

I was still running away, trying to escape those memories, the anguish, and my history, when the neighbours noticed how bloodied my hands were. They were staring at me as I was running. I've been running since I was 18.

I was just 18***still a kid trying to enjoy my life, trying new things, I was just 18 when my world turned upside down. I was just 18 and I was already running away from everything.

But I knew there were people like or maybe still younger than me that were running away too in this society, who were running away in their nightmare.

The world was too cruel for us, too cruel that teens like me considered suicide as the answer to our problems.

In fact, it cannot be solved, we just passed down our problems to our parents or to the people who we left behind, to the people who mourn for our death, to the people who once hated us. We just made our escape, and now I can finally understand why most teenagers tries to take his/her life away. I could finally understand why he took his life away.

It was midnight when I reached my objective, the bridge, the bridge that brought me the happiest memories but later turned devastating ones. I yelled, "Fuck!" as my knees started to tremble.

I cried even louder, "Fuck those monsters."

Fuck that abuser, fucking him who caused me too much pain, him that made me want to take my life away him that killed me two years ago, him who caused me so much trauma and nightmare i badly want to escape, him–the reason why I'm scared of being touch.

"Miss!"

I was yanked away by someone, crap. I'm not looking to be saved! I want to go away.

I screamed, "Fuck, get off me!" as I rose up and turned to face the person pulling me. He was dressed in a black leather jacket with a white shirt underneath, a white mask.

I tried to commit suicide, I tried to take the life I wish I never had.

I'm not in need of their pity.

I gave him a frigid look as he lectured, "You're wasting your life just because you have problems, think about those people who want to live but can't because they have to endure something!"

Damn, I am tired of this life.

I sneered, "Then they can have my life," and started to back away. Just as I was about to fall to the ground, he caught me and held me, and for the first time in two years, I no longer felt afraid to be touched.

He yelled "Help!" and I heard some footsteps before I eventually closed my eyes and fell asleep.

***

White walls, a white door, a woman injecting something into me while wearing a mask and a white skirt and top.

I'm not sure where I am. This is not how my room appears; I don't like how the white colour makes the space feel empty. I can see an oxygen tank next to me; am I going to die? Where am I, why do I have an oxygen tank, and why? I'm not at home, so it can't be someone else. Did the guy I met last night bring me here?

The nurse acknowledged and grinned, "You're awake."

Obviously, I am awake, my eyes are wide open duh!

"Doc. August. your patient is awake." she spoke on what the hell, it looks like a microphone but it isn't a microphone, ugh! How do I explain it? and where's the guy wearing all black, he really looks creepy last night. but he made me realise something.

I shouldn't waste my life over my problems, and that I should think that they are people dying because of sickness but want to live longer so I decided to give my heart and other internal organs to those people who need it.

To those people out there looking for a donor, I am willing to be the donor.

I turned to face the man standing next to me and said, "Hello, Miss." He was sporting a stethoscope and a white coat.

I sternly said, "Paris Maverick Prescott, you can call me Mave or Paris."

He laughed.

He glances through the documents he was carrying "So, how's my condition?" I sarcastically asked

"I recommended you to a psychiatrist, you tried to commit suicide last night, Ms."

"So what?"

"You need help, Paris." he let out a deep sigh

"Fuck that, I don't need your help, I don't need your fucking help!"

"But—"

"Me? Comitting suicide is none of your business."

"Ma'am. I am just helping you get the treatment you need."

"I don't need any of your bullshit help."

"Paris–"

"Just stop, your help won't matter, your help won't help me because you cannot help a person who can't even help herself, you can't help a person who can't help me not because i don't want you too but because I can't even help myself, how can you help me if I can't even stand in my feet being brave to face those nightmares? How can you help me when I already considered running away?"

The doctor sighs looking defeated and adds, "Someone called the hospital last night and the team arrived-you were lying on the ground, unconscious."

"I can't get in touch with your mother, and your bills are paid."

"Wait, wait, what? I was fucking alone when you arrived?" the doctor slowly nodded, looking at me puzzledly.

"Yes, Ma'am." he responds.

"But I was with someone last night, and he was dressed in a black leather jacket with a white shirt underneath, as well as a black cap and a face mask. He had this manly voice-an angelic voice perhaps."

"Ma'am, I assure you, you were the only one there when the team and I arrived." I nodded slowly before turning my back on him. He was present, and when he hugged me last night, I felt different. He took my fears away, and for a little while, I felt protected.

I'd like to know his name and who he truly is.

"Do you have any parents or guardians we could contact?" the Doctor inquired.

My mum is aloof. I faced him and shook my head slowly, my jaw gritted, Parents? hahaha. I never had parents

"All right, I'll be right back."

"Wait a minute, do you-"

"What?"

"Do you have a patient in need of a heart donor?"

He questioned, "Why?"

I wish to carry out a good deed before I pass away.

I want to give someone a life, a life I never had. Even if I had this heart and it was still beating, I couldn't accept the reality that I would spend my entire life living in my nightmares.

I cried out in desperation, "I just want to, I want to give them a chance at living for***"

"We do have one patient who needs to find a donor by the end of the month or he would-you know," he stated with agony. I guess this man is really close to the patient because he talks about something that could happen to them in the future.

I questioned out of curiosity, "Were you close to this person?"

"He was like a brother to me," he remarked before opening and heading out the door. The nurse followed him and closed the door.

If it's his best buddy, I'm willing to be the donor for as long as he lives, but first I want to get to know him. I'd like to tell him to look after my heart. This heart, which was in a lot of agony before,

I hope the next owner won't hurt it as much as I did.

He better take good care of this helpless heart, I hope.

Chapter 2

The nurse softly announces, "Miss, I'll be the one to clean your wounds in your arms." She had prepared some betadine, a bandage, a gauze pad, and a plaster. Maybe it was the wound I got from cutting my wrist.

"What's your name?" I asked, smiling.

"Cariona, an OJT nurse here."

"Nice name, I'm Paris, goodluck with your OJT, Cariona," I uttered smiling

She grinned at me and said, "And, if you're really willing to donate your heart to someone who needs it, please go to Doc. August's office, they're waiting for you." I allowed her to treat my wounds and nodded slowly before she helped me inside the doctor's office.

We went inside. I believe that this is just the hospital room with the black door; the wallpaper depicted a galaxy in space, with planets all around the room. Perhaps the doctor was an astronaut.

"Where are we? This doesn't look like Doc. August office."

"Oh no, Doc. August specifically told me that we should go directly to this room, I forgot to tell you, I'm sorry."

"So where are we?"

"In someone's room, the patient needs a heart donor."

Oh, so we are in the astronaut's room, kidding. but I love how they decorated this place, ah wish they also decorated mine.

"Oh so you have arrived." someone spoke in my back, I turned against him, he was wearing hospital pajamas, he was also holding a book***it kinda looks fantasy based on the book cover.

"Hi."

"I am Spencer Thaddeus Martin," he introduced himself, he must be the owner***patient of this room.

He offered his hand for a handshake but I refused to shake his hand. I don't like handshakes nor physical touches by men.

"Paris." I coldly stated before looking again at the room

"So you like fantasy books?"

"Yeah." he simply answered as he put back the book on his small bookshelf

"So you need my heart." I say.

"Yes," he simply says.

I let out a deep sigh, maybe the black guy was right, there are people out there who want to live but don't have the power to do so.

But I can give them my life, I can give them a chance to live on, a chance to live the life i never live.

A life I never had.

I honestly can't die without having a little fun and without accomplishing my Dad's bucket list, despite the fact that I absolutely wanted to die.

"Okay, then I'll give you mine, I'll give it to you in one month, give me one month then you can have my heart."

I sat on his bed and stared up at him; I continued to do so when I stood up. "But I do have one request," I said.

"Take care of my heart" oh my innocent heart.

"I will, I will take good care of it." he smiled, i smiled back before standing up.

"I should go now."

"Wait."

"Hmmm?"

He took a step forward to me, he stopped when he was 5 step apart

"I have one request too, let's be friends." I slowly nodded. "Friends but no physical touches." I smiled.

I fulfilled a goal on my father's bucket list by making a buddy!

He suggests, "Hey, how about we go to lunch together?"

I grinned as I stepped out and replied, "Okay, let's have lunch as friends." It was still early in the morning, so I went back to my room to get some sleep.

How should I cross everything off my dad's bucket list of goals in 30 days?

BUCKET LIST WITH MY DAUGHTER

1. Make friends with other kids

I smiled as I put a check on it, 9 more things to do, then I'm good to go.

***

"You fell asleep." A guy spoke, I opened my eyes and saw Spencer sitting in the chair, his face was closed to me, I could feel his breathing, his lips turned pale when he noticed how close he was to me.

"You're too close Spencer, no physical touches remember?" he was getting closer to me like we are about to kiss each other

He stumbled and blurted out "Uh, sorry." I smirked and asked, "I'm sorry too, what time is it?"

"I've been patiently waiting all afternoon for you; it's dinnertime."

"You didn't show up," he sulked. charming, that made me giggle.

"I'm sorry, let's go."

With so many unanswered questions on his face, he asked, "To where?" with a furrowed eyebrow.

"Dinner."

Don't you dare say you had dinner already?

"I didn't; on the contrary, I waited for you to get up so that we could eat dinner together. I had already placed our food order."

I was excited since eating is where I feel most at ease.

I questioned, "What did you order?"

"Pizza, two improbable hamburgers, two large fries, and a litre of coke."

I grinned gleefully. We should head to your space room.

He extended his hand to me, drawing my attention to the line tattoo on his arm.

"There will be no physical touches, such as holding hands."

His hands clenched into fists and he said, "Yeah, right."

"Let's go," he said, biting his bottom lip and marching off. Nevertheless, he is gentle and does not possess a monster-like demeanour.

He must be a big fan of the cosmos based on his universe-themed room. Just like how I like death and grim-reaper a lot

"So you like space or the galaxy." It's a sentence that sounded like a question.

"No I love it......because whenever I look at them I feel safe, Galaxy is my escape."

"Why? Why would you claim that the cosmos is your heaven? My eyebrows furrowed and looked deeply into his eyes.

"Because whenever I feel suffocated about my sickness, looking at the stars gives me hope, looking at the moon gives light to my dark world."

I stared at him, and he gazed at me with his captivating eyes, saying, "I see." We seemed to be longtime friends as we exchanged looks. His attention was diverted as his phone rang.

"Oh it's the delivery rider, I'll go get our food, you go sit there." he pointed to the chair near the window, I sat on the chair by the window and stared out the window where I could easily see the city lights as I said, "Okay take care." I have never witnessed this kind of beauty before

"City lights, beautiful," Spencer spoke

"It really is."

"Oh let me help you."

"No, sit down," he commanded.

"Okay." As he opened the back of the pizza and poured my glass with coke, I once again peered out the window as he prepared our dinner.

"Is it okay if I sit here?" I nodded, I grabbed a slice of pizza and let myself devour the impossible burger.

"You must be that hungry, you didn't eat all day." he snapped.

I laughed at him, he was right, I didn't eat anything the whole day, I slept a lot.

"So what are you gonna do in one month?" he asked

"bucket list." I replied

"Bucket List?"

"My dad created a bucket list that I should complete before he died."

"So that's why."

"Yeah."

"So why did your dad die?" he asked, he looked at me innocently as he had no idea what he asked me.

"Just don't asked,"

"Are you alone in this space room?"

"Ah yes,"

"Where's your parents?"

"Mom was too far away, Dad was busy with work, they could only visit me once a month, Paris."

"Oh."

"And you? What brings you here?" he asked curiously.

"I***I tried committing suicide last night then I met a guy, a guy who saved me from my misery, the guy who escaped with me, the guy who called ambulance but left me alone in that cold street."

We stayed silent seconds after that, I let out an awkward laugh.

We let ourselves devour our food, it tooks us an hour to finish everything,

"Let's complete the bucket list together."

Chapter 3

My smile disappeared in an instant as I heard him say that he doesn't need to be with me completing my bucket list. I can do it alone.

I put down the glass of coke I was drinking and stood up, "Thank you for the dinner." I coldly said before walking away and slammed the door on my way out.

"Paris, wait." he chase, I stopped when he pulled me my arms,

"I told you no touching!" I shrieked

He slowly let go of me as I swallowed a big lump in my throat

"What?" I asked

"Look, if ever I've said something that offended you, I'm sorry."

Argh, i hate those puppy eyes people gave me, i gave in easily but not this time, no.

Being soft is where it got me here in the first place.

"You didn't do something just...leave me alone." I said he let go of my arms, I bowed down my head before turning my back against him before walking away.

"Paris—"

"Please.."

"Okay, good night, Paris." I heard him say this before I closed my door.

"Good night, Spencer." I whispered "Sweet dreams, dear friend."

***

"You can leave the hospital now," the doctor said while the nurse was cleaning my wounds. I smiled bitterly before nodding.

"I'm still going to donate my heart, doc."

Doc. August gave the warmest smile before leaving my room. I did not bring anything except for my wallet that had my bucket list and Dad's picture. I wore the outfit that I wore before I got into this situation. Oh the guy with black outfit, I want to thank him but also slap him for leaving me alone there.

"So you're leaving?" Spencer……

"Don't worry, I'll be back."

"You know, I could be with you doing the bucket list … .just to watch over you, you might ruin the heart before giving it to me." he snickered, I rolled my eyes at him before walking out, sulking.

"Paris, please."

What a pity, "fine,"

His eyes were filled with joy and excitement, "I'll be back tomorrow, we are going to Paris, France. Give me your phone, I'll write down my number, chat with me, tonight." I smirked before grabbing his phone, I jotted down my number before giving it back to him.

"Paris?" Spencer arched an eyebrow

"Yes, Paris, let's go there and do some adventure, especially Skydiving."

After which, I visited the bridge where I met him…the black guy, I might run into him or meet him again here, I was hoping*** to meet him again.

I got home disappointed after an hour of hanging on that bridge, he wasn't there … .he wasn't on the bridge today. Maybe he was gone. I was standing in front of a big blue gate, the house after entering this gate wasn't the house I could call home, my room I couldn't call my comfort zone. I sighed deeply before pressing the doorbell, I pressed it a few times before my mom came out.

"Paris." she worriedly called, she pulled me for a hug, a mother's hug, i've been longing for.

"I'm sorry, I made you worry," I wail like a baby as I buried my face in his shoulders.

"Mom, I'm***sorry."

"Shhh it's okay baby." she caressed my back as I sobbed.

"I'm sorry***"

"Shhhh, let's go inside and talk this one out, I love you, paris. Stop crying." she let go of me before giving me a kiss on the forehead.

"I'm sorry too," she said. We sat on the couch, she already commanded our maid to give me a glass of water.

"For what?" I asked the maid to give me the glass and I gladly accepted it.

"For" she let out a deep sigh "Everything."

"And for not telling you something about you."

"Tell me what?"

My mom's lips parted "about your dad's***." she whispered the last words that I couldn't hear.

"Huh? Dad's what?" I query.

"Nevermind, uh, do you plan this weekend?"

"Oh, yes, I'm flying to Paris."

"Do you have money?" oh fuck, i do not.

"Okay, I know that face of yours, I'll send you later on, go and have fun in Paris, sweetie."

"Pack your things and oh do you have an acquaintance?"

"Yes, I do have."

"A friend?"

"Yes."

"A boy?" she teases

"I'll see you later."

I smiled at her before saying goodbye, because I needed to clean my room because it was filthy and bloody. My room is so dirty, with clothing all over the place, shattered glass, and blood all over my bed that I sighed deeply as I entered and shut my doors. After putting my hair in a sunflower-patterned hair tie and scooping up my phone from under the bed to attach it to my headphones so I could listen to my favourite music, I started gathering my clothing and placing them in the basket.

"This is going to be a long day." I bit my lower lip and chuckled. After picking out my clothes, I put them in my laundry before cleaning my bloody restroom.

It took me two hours to finish cleaning my room. I already finished folding my clothes, I also prepared my luggage which has my sweater, coats, my Paris hat, dress, skirt, pants, high heels and boots, and toiletries.

Past six o'clock when my phone vibrated

UNKNOWN:

HEy, it's Spencer, what time are we going to the airport tomorrow?.

PARIS:

Oh, 4 in the morning, have you

Packed?

SPENCER<3:

AH, yes.

I was waiting for him***for Spencer, the last time he chatted was 2 hours ago, I have to rebook a flight, argh!

PARIS:

Where are you?

A few moments had passed and still no reply for him***I guess he wouldn't come, so I started walking away.

"Hey."

Spencer….he came, he was trying to catch his breath when I looked at him, he looked tired. I rushed directly to him and stopped when I was close to him, he was sweating. He smiled before giving me a bouquet of sunflowers.

"Why are you late?" I asked.

"I'm sorry, I just had an emergency."

"Oh, and sunflowers ."

"...my favourite***how did you know?"

"Your necklace, your hair tie and your wallet."

"Pft, let's go." I sounded annoyed but to be honest, I felt a weird feeling. A feeling I never felt before.

I sighed deeply before grabbing my luggage and walking beside him.

I took the window seat while he sitted in the sit right next to me, he fell asleep when he just sitted there 5 minutes ago

"What took you so long?" I asked the sleeping manly beauty Spencer Thaddeus.

I looked at him. Why Spencer? Why did it take you 2 hours to arrive when the hospital was just a 30 minute drive?

Chapter 4

Ah, here we are in Paris. It's already 9 in the morning here and we booked one room but 2 beds***2 single beds.

We were now strolling in the streets to buy some refreshments before visiting the Eiffel tower.

"Uh, let's buy some pastries and shake?"

"Yeah, let's go."

We entered a cafe, it had this minimalistic ambiance that attracted me, it had this big glass case holding the pastries and oh the smell of coffee, they're only a few people here on their laptops working.

"One pain au chocolat, and uh a strawberry milkshake." I glanced at Spencer who was busy looking at the menu board.

"Uh, a piece of a chocolate cake and a grape milkshake." he smiled at the cashier, he took a few bucks from his pocket, he said he will pay for our food.

"Merci, monsieur, madame." the waitress said as she handed us our orders.

I smiled at her and waved goodbye, she waved back.

"So where are we going now?" Spencer asked and took a sip from his milkshake.

"Eiffel Tower."

"Oh my! That's my dream destination."

 "Really?"

"Yeah, and I'm glad I visited the city of love with you." he glanced at me, mesmerization visible in his eyes.

"Yeah." We both ran off like a kid, laughing at each other, enjoying the moment that won't last forever.

SPENCER POV.

I hope I can stop time so I can keep this moment forever, But deep inside me I already, I couldn't.

I knew I couldn't live in this moment forever.

PARIS POV

"I love Paris."

"I love you, Paris." Spencer shouted, maybe to so much happiness, he held me, his arms, i've been longing, is he the black guy? His arms felt safe, he held me like he was willing to be my escape when I'm misery.

Everything stops when my eyes meet him. For the second time in 2 years, I let a man touch me, held me. I smiled at him as our bodies collided, we hugged under the eiffel tower, this is one of the best memories i've ever had.

My eyes remained looking at him, remained looking at the guy who made me safe, looking at the guy that will own my heart,

"That was fun." he commented when we got back to our hotel.

"Yeah, it was fun." I chuckled and gave him the sweetest smile I could ever give.

"I'm sorry I broke the rule." he apologetically said.

"What rule?"

"No physical touches."

"Spencer….."

"I know and I'm sorry."

"Hey, it's okay, you can touch me, you can hold me, you can hug me." I walked down closer to him and let myself embrace him with open arms.

"Can I kiss you?" he asked

I glared at him which made him laugh

"It's okay,"

His breath was getting heavier and heavier. "Are you okay?"

"Do you have something like an inhaler or what?" I panicked, he pointed out his bag, I hurriedly grabbed it and made a huge mess just to get the inhaler.

"Here." he took it from my hand.

"You need to rest, I will just go and take***a shower."

"Okay," he took a deep breath before laying down.

I entered the bathroom and let out a deep sigh as I looked at myself in the mirror, I am wearing a grey sweater.

I put my hair in a messy bun and started washing my face.

I got out of the bathroom, and decided to go out;church is the first thing that comes to my mind.

"Please let him."

"Please let him live for a month, with that heart." I swallowed a big lump in my throat.

"After a month he can live with him carrying my heart and my spirit being with him."

Begging is not my thing 2 years ago, but for Spencer*** I would kneel on God just to save Spencer.

"Please god, please.."

***

When I got back to the hotel, I took a shower. I let my body be wet by the water, thinking of what could happen tomorrow?

Skydiving….

He was sleeping peacefully when I stepped out from the bathroom, I stepped out wearing my pajamas, of course!

I glanced again at Spencer before slowly closing the door;walking through the hallway, I want to see the things he admires the most***stars.

I took the elevator to the 12th floor then stairs to the rooftop, the wind hugged me filling me with calm and serenity when I arrived. It was beautiful, I could see the Eiffel Tower.

"I wish he was here." but he's asleep and he needs to rest.

"Beautiful."

I looked at the view for a few more minutes before deciding to go back. I was about to leave the rooftop when an unknown caller called.

"Hello?"

"This is Doc. August, how's Spencer."

"He's doing good."

"Oh great, please tell him to drink his medicine, I don't want to see him suffer like how I saw him a day ago."

"What do you mean?"

We talked for a few more minutes, I held my tears.

"Okay, thank you."

I knelt to the ground gripping my pajama, "Please, not now!" I said sobbing while looking at the sky, what a beautiful sky.

"Please." my heart aches in too much pain

"Please, don't take him away from me."

"Let him live!" I shouted.

"You can't just take him away from me after giving him to me."

"You can't just take him away." I lowered my head, neck appearing to shrink.

"Please***let him live." my chin trembled as I ran back to our hotel room, crying.

He was late that day not because he got stuck in the traffic or wanted to make fun of me or had an emergency, he was late because he almost died because of a heart attack.

"Damn, I should've known." I rushed. I opened the door and saw Spencer still sleeping, I covered my mouth so he wouldn't hear me.

"Why him?"

Chapter 5

"Your eyes it's swollen and red." he commented and looked through my eyes.

He just woke up and he noticed my eyes immediately.

"Oh, I couldn't sleep last night, my eyes will look like this if I don't sleep." I lied

"Did i made you feel uncomfortable?" he worriedly asked, brows wrinkle as he walked closer to me and sitted beside me in the beige couch.

"Of course not." I defended

"Hey, you can tell me everything, you know." he smiled and gave me a hug,

Why does the kindest person in the world have to die first?

Why can't god take those people who were bad, assholes perhaps***for example my step-dad.

"Hey why are you crying?" he ask and wipe my tears

"I'm sorry."

"I'm sorry Spencer."

"Hey, stop crying, what's wrong?"

"Nothing, I often get emotional." I let go of him and wipe my tears

"Oh, stop crying now, let's go and check that bucket list of yours." he stood up and offered me his hand, I gladly accepted it.

***

"Wear your parachutes." the captain commanded, we followed him and wore our glass and parachutes.

"Here we go." We jumped as I held Spencer's hand.

"Woohoo!" he exclaimed, please let it be the way, here I am wishing to stop time to be in this moment forever.

—

"Ah, that was amazing."

"I know right."

"Thank you for being here, Spencer."

"I'll always be here, Paris." I smiled bitterly but I wouldn't be Spencer, I would eventually leave.

"Let's go, flight's tomorrow. We have to rest and pack."

I let him hold my hand, we looked like girlfriend and boyfriend on a date, lol, what am i thinking?

"Can I lay by your side?"

We were on the rooftop looking at stars.

"Yes."

He then lay down by my side. "It's beautiful up here." I looked up at the stars.

"Yeah."

SPENCER POV.

I am looking at the most beautiful thing in the world Paris***Maverick Prescott. She was so busy looking at the stars that she didn't notice I was looking at her. Am i inlove with her?

She only sees me as her friend that would always be there for her.

Chapter 5

TW: just a warning!

I shouted when I got back home, ah i miss this house, well technically the house not the memories i had here.

"You're finally home." Mom spoke, she was walking downstairs towards me,

"Mommy, I snickered and ran to her.

"Welcome home, sweetie." she said and hugged me with open arms.

"Now, this is home."

"Welcome home, honey." a manly voice spoke, that voice that made my spine shivers, it's been so long since I last heard it.

"Ti–tito An–anton."

"Hello hija," he smiled, that fucking smile i fucking hated.

"Mom, why is he here?" I asked without breaking my stare at Anton's.

"We got back together."

W-what? That guy is living here with us again…. That guy who molested me.

"Disgusting," I mouthed, fucking disgusting Anton, his lips quivered, I swallowed hard, glared at him. "I'll just go upstairs." i say before kissing Mom's cheek and running to my room, I want to rest, after this I'll be with Spencer, I don't want to be stuck here with that disgusting asshole.

I slammed my door as I leaned on it, tears started to fall as those memories came rushing back, replaying what had happened 2 years ago.

"Stop, please make it stop, stop fucking remembering those things, please." my voice broke, I can't handle it, please make it stop. Damn.

With shaking hands, I called the guy who made me safe.

"Sp–spencer." I said trembling, I took a deep breath.

"Who the fuck made you cry? Where are you Paris?"

"Stay there in the hospital, I'll go there. Just stay there, I need you."

"Okay, I'll be here, tell me everything, let me be your escape, Paris."

I ended the call and ran through my closet and grabbed my Dad's hoodie, I picked up my wallet and car keys, before storming out.

"Where are you going?" Mom asked when she saw me in a rush.

"Escaping." I smiled at her, my swollen eyes met hers as I ran through the door, I entered my car and drove briskly to the hospital, it was only 20 minutes away.

He was waiting for me outside when I got there. I parked my car and ran to him, he extended his arms as I got closer and pulled me for a hug, "Shhh, it's okay." I started crying again….please let's get out of here, help me stay away from the monster…..

"Yes, let's escape together in this miserable world."

SPENCER POV

We were driving to some place away from here, I don't care what Paris would say, but she needs to breathe.

I was planning to go to my hometown, Baguio, Philippines. I dialed Dad's number and told him I am going to use the jet plane. I am a pilot***if only my condition wasn't the problem I would be flying in the sky right now.

"You sure?" he asked. I nodded slowly even though he couldn't see me but he knew my silence would always mean 'yes.'

"Okay, just be careful, I don't want you to get hurt, son."

"Yes pa." I smiled and ended the call

I drove to the airline and they immediately assisted me.

Paris hates to be touched by men. That's why I didn't let them touch her, I carried her and secured her first before securing myself.

I put headphones on her and she didn't even wake up, she was too asleep, she was asleep the whole ride.

"Captain, are you sure about this? You might get a heart attack up there."

I immediately took a glance at Paris, "Yes, as long as I'm with her."

"Your girlfriend?" he asked and looks at Paris, I glared at the guy

"No, she's my wife."

—

"This is Capt. Spencer speaking, we are ready for departure."

"We are heading for take-off."

I took a deep breath and took a glance at Paris before looking back at the runaway.

"Paris 311, runaway 11, you are cleared for takeoff." I smiled as we took off, I miss flying with the sky, I miss flying with clouds. I miss this.

Chapter 6

Tw: Warning This Chapter Had Some Ehem Ehem Scenes

"Welcome to Baguio, Sir." an old lady welcomed me, I rented a car while we were still in the US, so it won't be hard you know.

And it's freaking cold here, "A sweater." I say we didn't bring anything, I had to buy at least a sweater for both of us, I'll take her to the mall later and go shopping.

"Are you a foreigner?" she asked, I nodded slowly. "2 sweaters for me and my wife." I said, she instantly nodded and left me in the cashier as my eyes looked through the whole store.

"Here, it's a couple sweatshirt." She gave me the sweatshirt who had a design of Mr and Mrs. "You have a beautiful wife, btw."

I grinned, "Yeah, she sure is, she's a wonderful person too but too bad she's asleep right now."

"And because you have a beautiful wife, you can have that sweatshirt for free."

"Oh no, I'll pay." I insisted and grabbed some money in my pocket. "No, you keep it and ask your wife on a date in a diner." she says, I shyly smiled at her before grabbing the sweaters and bid my goodbye before going back to the car.

"Hey." Paris said with a serious look.

"Hey,"

"Where are we?" she asked

"Baguio, Philippines." I said gritting my teeth

Her mouth fell open, I smirked at her before starting the car and drove to a 5 star hotel.

"Thank you for escaping with me, Spencer." the corner of her mouth rose up and smiled slightly in a smile.

Paris was in the passenger seat, holding my hand. I smiled and brushed a strand of hair from her face, she smiled back at me as I leaned in closer and closer to her.

"You're making me crazy over you, Paris." there's this butterfly that i have been feeling in my stomach, I look directly in her eyes before my eyes look at her lips, her pinkish pouty lips.

My heart was pounding like I was about to have a heart attack, I caressed her cheek before pressing my lips against hers, as I let go, she pulled me for another, unlike earlier this kiss was passionate, heated.

"You're making me crazy too, Spencer." she smiled, "I love you, Paris. And I am not forcing you to say I love you too, I'll wait until you're ready to say it." I gave her an assuring smile as I stepped out of the car and offered to open the car door for her.

"Let's get one room and share the bed, if that's okay with you." Naughty Paris.

"Yeah." I held her hand before entering the hotel, thank god, they're not full so we got the suites.

We got our suites as I pulled her for a hug, "I'll be your escape Paris," I says

"Yeah." she seductively said, I pinned her against the wall and I kissed her hungrily as she wrapped her arms around my neck. We kissed and walked until we were both in bed hungry kissing each other, when I let go we were both breathless.

"Own me, Spencer, fuck me." she says before pulling me for another kiss, I remove my lips on hers before removing my clothes and hers. My kisses went down to her neck as she moaned my name, she arched his neck to give me more access, I removed her bra and sucked her nipple like a hungry child craving for her milk.

"Spencer, ah!" she moaned as my kisses went down to his tummy; I removed her panty and sip her clitoris, She's fucking wet, I let my toungue explores her pussy. "Spencer, fuck me more." She grabbed my hair as she pushes my face more.

"Let me suck your dick." she seductively said before getting up and pushed me to the bed, I let her remove my boxer as my big boy came out being erotic and getting ready for a war. She took a deep breath before giving me a blowjob, she licked the top of my dick as she let my dick enter her mouth.

"Fuck, Paris." I moaned as my head went up, it was fucking too yummy, and she was sexier down there.

—

"Enter me," she says as she leads my erotic manhood to her wet pussy, "Ah." I moaned she was fucking tight. "Fuck." she whispers as tears start to fall.

"Hey, what's wrong?"

"Nothing, please fuck me harder, make me forget what happened to me 2 years ago?" she begged as I thrust through her surely but deeper.

"Hmm, Spencer, shit. Faster!"

"Ypu're fucking tight baby, but I'll fucking make sure, You're gonna need a wheel chair after this." I huskily said before holding her breast and thrust harder, "Oh fucking shit, that's it, fuck."

"Moan my name, Paris, shout my name, moan it." I said as I let myself devour her nipples.

"Ah, fucking Spencer, Spencer ah fuck deeper baby, deeper."

I removed my penis from her as I told her to turn her back against me, as I pulled her hair and entered my pet. As I slapped her buttcheeks.

"Fuck, Paris." I moaned

"I'm cumming!" I thrust more and cum inside her before claiming her lips.

—

"Do you want to eat or take a shower?" I asked, we were in bed cuddling and still naked.

"I want both," she replied and hug me more

"Okay, then I'llstay here then I'll prepare the bathtub and while you're in there I'm gonna order us some food then if you want we'll go outside, it's still afternoon."

"Yeah let's go."

Just like I've said I prepared the bathtub for her they have some scented candles here so I grab one***the sunflower one.

"The bathtub is ready."

"Okay wait,"

"No, I'll carry you." I said before carrying her like a bride, I slowly put her on the bathtub and kissed the top of her head. "What do you want to eat?" I asked

"Any Filipino food."

"Okay, then I'll order Bulalo and Adobi then rice." she nodded slowly before she let her body soaked down.

***

The food was already here, I also had plans for today like buying stuff and strawberries and make strawberry shake***Paris's favourite.

"Hey," I looked at her, she was wearing just a robe and fuck she looks so fucking hot. "Can you wear the sweatshirts and the pants you wore earlier? I didn't buy his clothes, we're just gonna go and buy them after we eat."

"Yeah, I can." she smiles before picking up her clothes on the floor, she comes back 5 mins later wearing her jeans and she's ready to eat.

I put some adobo on a bowl and bulalo, and also put rice on her plate and utensils. I also poured water on his glass, "Let's eat."

"Hmmm, wow, this adobo tasted so fucking good." she says she tastes a spoonful of rice with a piece of pork on top.

"So, what's next on your bucket list?" I asked her and took a sip of the bulalo.

"Forget about the bucket list, Let's create our own memories without the bucket list."

"Then don't give your heart to me, Paris, I can find someone else's heart, I cannot live without you, I can't live without you, baby." I softly said before holding her hands, "Spencer, no, what if you can't find someone in time?"

"Then live without me, live for me."

"Then, that's unfair. You said you can't live without me so I shouldn't give you my heart."

"But what about me? What about me Spencer? I cannot live without you too, so you can't die, you can't die."

"Paris…"

"No. that's fucking unfair, if you don't want me to give you my heart then atleast let me help." she sighs before she stood up and knelt while still holding my hand.

"Please, don't be unfair."

"Please." she looks down as i looked at her,

"Shh, come here," I pulled her up and hugged her. "Okay, as you wish, my Queen."

She smiled sweetly at me before pinching my nose "Good and I should be your one and only Queen," she chuckles, ah her sweet cute chuckles.

"You're the only one baby," I smiled as I let our nose collided

"I love you, Paris." I sweetly smiled against her lips.

"I know."

"Let's finish our food then let's go shopping at the mall, 50/50."

"No. My Queen ain't gonna spend some money." I seriously said, we continued eating and talking nonstop.

***

"Oh, a local store, we might have something to buy there, so let's go inside?"

"Well, as long as My queen wants it then we'll get it,"

We entered the shop and roamed around, they're were many souvenirs and sweaters here for couples. They were also selling strawberries and jams. They have lots of stuff here, "Oh I want this." Paris excitedly said and pointed out the strawberries with chocolate, "Then, let's get that." I grab one and put it in the cart and this, she says I chuckled as she put it in the cart, we shopped more for what Paris wants then what she gets.

"Bye, Ma'am , Sir."

We look for more shops with sweaters and jackets. "Oh, a couple night wears, let's buy them!!!" she ran like a kid when she saw that. She's cute.

"Oh god, the food here is so freaking good." she says as she takes a bite of Turon, "Let's just live here, Spencer."

"Yeah, let's live here, babe."

"Hey, you look like a goddess, can we take a picture with you?" A few people approached Paris, and Paris smiled awkwardly.

"I'm sorry but my wife here don't like to take pictures," I butt in

"Oh, okay, thank you, enjoy your vacation here." they said as they wave their hands

"Are you okay?" I softly asked

"Yeah, thank you."

"Anything for you."

"Let's go back to the hotel?"

"And make some miracles" she joked around but that fucking joke was said seductively.

"Kidding." she added

"Stop joking, you're gonna wake him." he said and pointed out on his dick

"Then, let's go to the hotel then let me wake him up." She smirked and entered the car, I grinned before opening my door and drove fast as soon as we reached the hotel room. Oh well, we did something again.

"Oh fucking Spencer, deeper, shit!" I cannot even see her pupils, I thrust harder and deeper just like what she said and for the second time I cummed inside her, we fucked until midnight, rested for a few hours then fucked each other again until well I bought a fucking wheelchair.

Just making sure, I'm gonna fuck her until she can no longer walked. "Ah shit!" I moaned. "Fuck you, Spencer, more."

Deeper and deeper until we reached

Chapter 7

Whoa! This is cool, this is one of my dreams to walk in the field of sunflowers.

"I'm glad you like it here."

"Thank you for bringing me here***"

"Spencer!" Someone called Spencer, it was a blonde hair girl with blue eyes, she's not that beautiful to be honest.

"Lina, hey." he says, that Lina girl ran towards him and hugged him tight, she didn't mind me as I was watching them with rage.

"Oh, who is she?" she asked as she pointed out her finger on me, I smiled wickedly as I got closer to her.

"WHo are you?" I ask back.

"Katalina Avrielle, Spencer's future wife, and you are?"

"Paris Maverick Prescott" I said

"Oh."

"Martin. I am not done yet lady, I am Spencer's wife so he doesn't need a future wife." I glared at her as I heard Spencer chuckles, "Yeah, she's right Lina, she's my wife."

"We'll go now, excuse us Lina." Spencer said and held my hands as we walked away from that ugly Lina girl.

"Where do you want to go next, wifey?" he asked in a silly way.

I glare at him

"You said earlier, you're my wife, woman,"

"Did I?"

"Jealousy, jealousy." he sang, as I slapped his arms

"I am not jealous."

"Yeah right." he chuckles as he looks at me straight in the eye

"So where do we go next?" he asked, I cheerfully smiled at him

"Can we go to the Mayon Volcano in Albay? I badly wanted to see that, they said it was the most beautiful volcano in the Philippines."

"Hmmm," he hummed

"Okay, as long as my wife wants it then let's do it." he beamed.

"Yehey!"

We walked through the hanging bridge, oh should I say he walked through.

I'm scared of heights, what if this bridge would fall down? Damn, my lips trembled as I took the first step.

"You can do it, baby!" he shouted in the other side, I closed my eyes as my shaking foot took another step, my breath was rapid, I took another step then another until I reached other side, I clung into Spencer, and embrace him for a hug, "I did it." I whispered, eyes brimming with happy tears.

"Yes, you did it, I'm so proud of you, now let's go and pack. We'll go to Albay."

I giggled as I held onto him as we walked, we enjoyed the day at that field buying everything, he also booked our flight while we were outside, some views are prosaic, but some views are worth appraising.

"So let's start packing," I opened our cabinet, we only bought a few clothes and this cabinet is capacious.

"Yeah, our flight is tomorrow around 9 in the morning so..we should leave the hotel around 6, and let's have breakfast on our way,"

"Okay then."

"What do you want to eat for breakfast?" my eyes gleam with joy as I squealed that made him laugh

"I want to try some silogs, I searched about it and it looks yummy, babe." I stopped for a second, "Did you just call me babe?" he curiously asked as he tilted his head.

"Hey, did you just call me babe?" he asked again and I stood there, pausing for a moment, did i?

"No!" I raised my voice and covered my mouth with my palm as my eyes widened with shock.

"I didn't call you, let's just pack our things" I cleared my throat as I started putting my clothes in the luggage Spencer bought.

He laughed but then he stopped as he held tightly on his chest, "I-I can't breath, P-Paris." I ran towards him and assisted him as I looked for his inhaler but I couldn't see it anywhere.

"Fuck." I cursed as I grabbed his phone and called 911.

"Hello, this is Paris Maverick Prescott—uh I have a patient here with heart failure, he cannot breath and I cannot find an inhaler somewhere, please bring one ambulance at Ariesotle Villa."

I ended the call, "Spencer, don't fucking close your eyes, fuck." I said loudly as I shook his body, he was slowly closing his eyes, the ambulance took a few minutes before arriving.

"No pulse."

A nurse was dragging me away from him, while they were busy saving him, I knelt on the floor as I prayed.

"Still no pulse, Continue CPR." the nurse said while doing CPR.

"Prepare to switch."

"Switch," then they gave 2 breaths, then another CPR but still got nothing, my body started shaking as they continued.

"He has a pulse now but still unconscious, let's bring him to the hospital."

I ride with the ambulance holding Spencer's hand, crying and kissing his hands, his cold fingertips match my watery one. We arrived at the hospital where they were running and I followed them.

"Please make him live, We'll go back to New York and after that we'll start the operation. Just please 3 more days, please let me be with him first for just 3 days." I whispered, they put some IVF on him, as they checked his heartbeat.

"He is okay now, may I know who you are and your relation to the patient?" The doctor who looked after him asked.

I let out a deep sigh as my lips put on a small smile "His fiancee."

"Paris Maverick Prescott, and soon to be Mrs. Martin, how is he doing, doc?"

"Unfortunately, he had a heart attack, he is dying, he needs a donor."

"The Donor, is in New York, doc. Is it okay if we go there, is he safe for travelling?"

"Yes, as long as some nurses would come to look after him." I smiled at him as I told him to give me the best nurses in the hospital. He picked 3 of them. I booked a private flight for us. I did go back to the hotel, to pack our things before going to the airport. Spencer was with the nurse on the way there, so I took a taxi.

I wore the sweater Spencer bought me on our way to the hotel, the sweater that had an MRS mark on it. I looked at the sky as I wondered what could our tomorrow be?

"Mrs. Martin, let's go." The flight attendant said as they grabbed my luggage, I thanked them as I walked out first, Spencer was already in the aeroplane with the nurse, I hired to look after him just like the Doctor said.

We arrived there earlier than expected; I ran through the halls of the hospital, I was looking for Spencer's doctor, Doc. August.

"Doc. August!" I shouted as I saw him checking on his files while walking down the hall, he waved his hand at me and smiled, his smiles slowly disappeared when he saw me almost tearing up, "Please save, Spencer." I held on to his hand as my tears started to fall. "Please save him, you can take my heart, just save him, please." I knelt down on him, he knelt down too as he was trying to make me stand up.

"Stand up, please." he say softly

"No, Please, Save him." I beg, "Please."

"We will conduct a test first, Paris, to see if you are compatible to be Spencer's donor." he said as I tried to stand up.

"I'll just go home, after the test Doc." I said.

"Take care, Paris." he says.

"I will, Doc. Please take good care of him when I'm gone."

"I will, Paris. I will take good care of your Spencer." My Spencer, it's good to hear it. He's my Spencer–the man I wanted to spend forever but sadly there's no forever in this world, nothing lasts in this world. We will eventually leave this horrible cruel world.

***

Staring at the sky while holding on the bridge railings, I am still hoping to find Mr. Black so I can say goodbye and thank you***because of him I met Spencer, Doc. August.

"I knew I would find you here." I looked around and saw him, the black guy, my jaw dropped as he removed his cap, his familiar scent that I smelled 2 hours ago, he folded his arms as he looked at me.

"Spencer, you-"

"Yes, I am, Mr. Black guy, the guy who stops you from jumping off the bridge." he said, tearing up.

"Thank you for saving me that day."

He tilts his head, a small smirk grows on his face.

"You're welcome. I love you, Paris."

"I know, Spencer."

We stayed there for a few more minutes, just staring at each other with admiration. I knew I loved him, but I'm having a hard time saying it.

"Let's go back to the hospital now, Spencer Thaddeus." I said as I walked closer to him and closed my eyes before colliding our lips.

"I love you so much, Paris."

"Thank you for loving me."

***

We both walked our way back to the hospital, it wasn't that far, though, we can walk our way there.

"Are you okay walking?" Spencer asked

"Yes, what about you?"

"I feel okay whenever I'm with you."

A small smile grew on my face as I clung to his arms and lay my head on his shoulder.

"I wish I could tell you how much I love you, Spencer." I whispered, just right for him to hear.

"I won't rush things with you, paris. I'll wait for you." he says back as he messes up my hair, I pouted and that made him laugh.

We walked and walked until we reached the hospital then another few minutes before reaching his room, Doc. August was already there including an old man with glasses, he kinda looks like Spencer, he must be Spencer's Dad.

"Hey, dad." Spencer let go of my hand and hugged his Dad, I smiled at them as I was about to go out, they can have their time.

"And where are you going, babe?"

"To give you space and time, love." I replied with a smile

"No, Ija, you stay here, I'll go now, I still have a flight on the way to the Philippines."

"Where in the Philippines, sir?" I asked, he might go to Baguio and I would just ask him to bring the strawberry jam, Spencer's favourite and my favourite.

"Cagayan De Oro."

"Oh okay, take care, sir." I bowed my head down as he walked away.

"Paris, let's talk to you." Doc. August seriously said, I nod at Spencer before Doc. August closed his door as we walked towards his office .Based on your test results.

"You possibly can't be Spencer's donor." he said in a low voice, my jaw dropped.

"Why?" I asked

"You have cancer, Paris." my world fell apart.

I took a step out still processing every words the doctor said, fuck.

I leaned my back against the wall as I let myself sit on the cold floor,

"It can't be"

"Damn, please." I sob while covering my face with my palm, I couldn't accept the fact that I am sick and I couldn't save Spencer. I can accept the fact that I am dying but the fact that I couldn't save him–the man who saved me, the man I love from the very beginning. The man I felt safe with.

"Are you okay?" Spencer asked as he leaned to the bathroom door. I nodded slowly before sitting in his bed.

"Did you cry?" he asked, I shook my head "No."

"Come here." he hugged me like a baby, then for a millionth time, I felt saved by an angel***an angel who also needs to be saved.

"I want to spend the rest of my life with you, Spencer." I whispered in his ears, he hug me tighter

"Me too, Paris." he snuck his face in my neck and smell me

"But we both know we can't, Spencer." I swallowed a big lump in my throat.

"And that's the most cruel thing ever."

"Why can't we just live a normal life without sickness and our mental health?"

"That's just how the world works, unfair, cruel."

"I want to give you the best life, Paris,"

"I want to give you a life where you can be happy and escape with those assholes, I want to give you everything. I want to give you the life you never had."

"I already spent that life when I was with you these days, when I was with you in Paris, in Baguio and here." I smiled bitterly as I remember those days where I was the happiest. Where he would just watch me being me

"I want to escape with you."

A tear escape from my eyes as I held his hand tight

"I want to live, I can't give you my heart." I let go of him before turning my back against him, I stood back and was about to walk out of this place.

"I don't need your fucking heart Paris." he seriously said, I turned my back and looked at him, he said it seriously but his eyes are about to cry.

"I need you, Paris, just you." he painfully said.

"I just need you to be with me, Paris, please." he knelt to the ground as he tried to hold my hand.

"You can have your heart but just be with me, please?" he says

"You always have me Spencer,"

"Then don't leave, stay with me in this empty room."

Chapter 8

"If I got to live, let's go visit The Philippine Volcano, the Mayon in Albay." he says as he plays with my hair, tangling it, we were both in bed cuddling with each other.

"Yeah, let's do that, so you should focus on doing well, hmmm." I said, tearing up.

"Paris,"

"Hmmm."

"If I do not wake up again, please take a good care of yourself,"

"You will wake up again, Spencer."

"That's just an 'if' Paris."

"I have so many what if's in my mind." he whispers

"What if i die?" he asked, my eyes watered as i think of an answer to his what if

"What if you got to live?" I ask back

"Then let's live happily, I'll try my best to make you happy."

"Then we will get married."

"Then have 5 or 3 kids."

"SPENCER!" I exclaimed

"What? Do you want 20 kids?" he tease

"SPENCER." I managed to look grumpy even though I'm already blushing on the inside.

"Kidding babe, but what about 30 kids?" he teased again

"Spencer, stop." I said irritatedly.

"Okay okay." he laugh

"I really want to spend my life with you, then we will be living in Baguio and go to Albay everytime you want,"

I looked at him, pain was visible in my eyes. "Me too, me too." I softly whispered as I let my lips pressed his.

"Paris, hmm" our faces drew from each other as I smiled at him, "I want to spend it with you too, Spencer."

"Paris, I don't have the ring right now or maybe we won't become boyfriend and girlfriend but will you marry me?" tears forms in his eyes as he looked at me, I bite my lower lip

"A forever with you?" I asked, his lips formed into a smile before nodding

"Then, it's a yes." I say before again and again kissing his soft lips.

"You know i love you but I love you more than you know." he started licking his lower lip.

"Yeah…."

We both talked about what we wanted to have in the

"Let's sleep now, Spencer." I said, it's late, and both of us are still awake.

"Good night, Spencer." I said as I cuddled into him.

"Good night, Paris, my Paris." I could feel his heart beating so fast like it was about to explode, "Your heart."

"It beats like crazy when I'm with you." he said as he hugged me more.

******

A glimpse of light woke me up by the morning, I smiled at my sleeping Spencer, my Spencer.

"Spencer." I called while caressing his face.

"Spencer," I called him again, I immediately stood up before pressing the blue button on the wall.

"Spencer, wake up." I said almost tearing up with shaky hands.

"Hey, wake up."

Realisation hit like a thousand knives stabbing my chest, the nurse then arrived, they were checking his vitals and administering drugs as they tried to save him with CPR and tried to save him again with AED.

The heart machine they connected to him was still beeping and it grew louder and frantic, Minutes had passed on as they stopped saving him, the doctor looked at me and slowly shook his head, "I'm sorry."

"I'm sorry, I couldn't save him."

"N-no." my voice cracked.

The doctor left me with Spencer's dead body, my chest tightens as I watch him sleeping.

"You're fucking unfair, Spencer." I whispered while crying.

I pressed my lips together as I touched his lips again.

"You said you cannot live without me, and I cannot live without you but why?"

"Why!" I screamed

"Spencer, please."

My knees broke down as I held my chest, Doc. August came, tearing up.

"Paris, Spencer wanted me to give you this." He handed me a red box and a letter, it was a beautiful ring. I cried violently as I hugged the box and the letter, with shaking fingers, I wore it.

Beforehand opening the letter.

Dearest, Paris.

My own person of city of love, I love you a lot, I wanted to spend my last remaining days with you being with me, I wanted to hold you, to kiss you so bad, i love you so much that did everything to gave you a reason to live even if that means, i'm going to die, you are special to me, Paris, So fucking special, that I watched you sleep as I wrote this letter, I'm glad that I am sick with this condition because if I am not sick, I wouldn't be close to you, I wouldn't end uo being your friend, your escape, I wouldn't end up falling for you, falling for you was the best decision I would never regret, I love you, my city of love, my Paris. For words could never capture the love I have for you, I would leave the world without hearing you saying I love you to me. I know this goodbye will be incredibly hard for you, but please know, I am always with you, Paris, I will always look out for you, again my love, I love you.

"Spencer." I tried to stood up as I went and hug him,

"I love you, Spencer."

"I already have said it, w-wake up now."

"Paris, y-you're bleeding." Doc. August said.

'N-no."

"N-no!"

"M-my angel," I cried my heart out

"You-you're pregnant?" Doc. August asked as I nodded my head.

"They're Spencer's babies—angel." I said sobbing

"Ahhhh!" I shouted, my knees weakened as my body collapsed, I heard August's voice before finally closing my eyes.

***-

5 days had finally passed since he passed away, and I am still living in the nightmare of his death. 5 days had passed since the love of my life left me. I sat on one of the chairs at his burial. We held a 10-day burial for him.

The priest who spoke earlier gets off the stage as his father tries to stop his sobs, he is hurting, just like me, he lost his son, the one and only Martin. I couldn't watch them bearing his agonising death.

"Hello, for all of you know, I am Frank Martin, Spencer's father, first of all, thank you for being here, for being with me, Spencer, and to my daughter in law***Paris." he looked at me as tears started to fell on his eyes, he looked up as he sniffle

"Spencer's my one and only son, he loves to play with aeroplanes, he loves to fly, but the thing he loves the most was the galaxy***the stars, the planets, the moon, we were doing just fine not until he collapsed."

He was telling the story of Spencer***what he likes or what he loves, or how they found out about Spencer's sickness.

"When we got into the hospital, the doctor said it was an heart attack, as a father it killed me knowing my son could no longer live a normal life, the doctor and i talked about the things to do and not to do, he was just 16, he was just 16 and he already suffered so much, Spencer was in and out to the hospital, it wasn't just heart failure, there's asthma."

"At the age of 23, We finally found a donor***Paris." I looked at him sadly as I wiped my tears in my eyes, I never cried right after I lost Spencer and my baby.

"They eventually became friends they travel together, I remember one time for the first time in 5 years, he let himself be free again, he let himself manipulate the engine of a jet plane again, it was my first time seeing my son being that happy,"

"They escaped together and came back here when Spencer had a heart attack, but sadly Spencer didn't want Paris to take her life away for him, he wanted Paris to live, he was so desperate that he kneeled in front of Dr. August gave any reasons to tell Paris that she couldn't do it."

"He passed away in the morning, he died in the arms of the woman he loved."

He gave me the microphone, I cleared my throat before smiling at them, but my tears were betraying me that my smile constantly disappeared

"I'm Paris, Spencer's city of love, being here today is killing me."

"It kills me because I couldn't imagine that I would be here now, attending the love of my life's funeral. He saved me the day I wanted to jump off that bridge, the day the man I was so afraid of came back, he saved me millions of times without even knowing it."

I glance at Spencer's urn

"You saved me but I couldn't save you and that's the worst part of loving you, You said you can't live without me so do i, but you left me, you left me without hearing the three words I badly want to tell you."

"You left me without hearing me say, I love you."

I heard the crowd sobs as I tried to continue my speech.

"Damn you, no matter how much I want to be mad at you, I can't."

"I have loved you desperately since the day I met you."

"Fly high with our dear angel, my love." The crowds looked at me poorly. That's right, I've lost the man that I love, and a baby in my tummy***the best gift I've ever had.

"I love you both, my dear angels.'

As I took my step down it was Doc. August turns to speak, to share.

"I'm August, Spencer's friend." he let himself introduced himself as he took a deep breath

"Spencer always wanted to be a pilot and I wanted to be a doctor, I reached our dream, Spence."

"I became Spencer's doctor and seeing him being in cardiac arrest or even having a hard time broke me."

He continued to speak as I stepped outside, I needed to breathe, this was suffocating me.

My knees were trembling as I walked my way out.

"Paris." Spencer spoke my name as I opened the door

"She was Spencer's city of love, She was Spencer's escape, Spencer's first and great love, Spencer's last." I looked at him, my eyes started to swell and I ended up crying there.

Chapter 9

PARIS POV

People come and go, and Spencer–left.

How pitiful of me hoping they stay, or should I say he would stay, life is sometimes unfair.

"Paris, it's time for your chemo." Doc. August said.

"I don't want to, bring me to the Philippines, can you?"

"Why? Is it because of Spencer?"

"Yeah, there's a place that we both want to go in that one very place in the Philippines."

"Where?"

"Mayon, I want to go to Mayon."

"Why there?

"Before Spencer was brought back to New York." I started off

"We were planning to go there, to Albay, to see Mayon."

"I was planning to say 'yes' to him there." I looked at the window as I said that.

I was planning to say 'yes' to him there, to be with him forever, to live with him until we both die or should i say until i die, without Spencer by my side, I had no more reason to live, no more reason to smile or to keep going through, to go under chemo. He was my life, Spencer was my life, I don't even know how to live my life anymore, I was always like this but not with Spencer–he taught me to live with him then he just left.

He made me realise that if I want to do something, I should do it now, because we don't know what's tomorrow or what our future holds. Do what you want to do now or regret it later.

"Okay, but promise me you will take the chemotherapy after this trip, okay?" he raised his pinky finger.

"Promise." as I raised mine.

Everyone in the hospital, when I say everyone***it's the Doctors and nurses here knows I hate being touched by men, so everytime they would send a female nurse or Doc. August, I trust him so he was the only man who touches me aside from Spencer.

"Thanks, August." I say

"You're welcome. Plan your trip now."He left me with a laptop. I immediately planned my whole trip. I was planning to stay there for the whole week, but 3 days is okay, 3 days is fine. After all, I would go alone on this trip. "Ah, Paris, you should bring one nurse to assist you if you need something, or if something happens." he barged in again, I nodded at him without even glancing at him.

I planned the trip and here I am on the plane. The nurse was beside me sleeping, just like Spencer, he sleeps when we fly together in Paris. He's cute.

When we arrived at Albay, I saw the Mayon up in the sky, it's beautiful, breath-taking, I've heard the legend of Panganoron & Magayon.

It is reported that she remains plagued by the men who loved her even in death and in another form. When Mayon is reported to explode, Panganoron is being tested by Patuga. But when Mayon is peaceful, Panganoron embraces her. Panganoron's tears fall as rain at times during his sadness.

Their story was sad, devastating, does loving can really kill someone?

Falling inlove was the best decision I've ever made. I used to say falling inlove is shit.

because being in love supposedly feels like everything. I enjoy the concept of love, but what about the notion of breaking up with someone I've fallen for? Oh no. I could never picture myself sobbing over a broken heart. Why would someone fall in love with the person who taught them a valuable lesson? Why do individuals fall in love with somebody they know won't reciprocate their feelings for them? I keep wondering why we must go through immense agony as a result of our great love in order to improve as human beings. Because heartbreak is a pain that may kill you, a suffering that I was experiencing every day, I question why people weep when they experience it.

I fell in love when I told myself not to, then I realised I fell in love many times but not with a person, but with something else; I fell in love with sunflowers, with Eiffel Tower, with stars, with Paris, France. With Mayon, Baguio, and the first person I fell in love with, the person I want to be with***Dad, and then Spencer.

What I have for Spencer wasn't a heart break, it was grief.

I was equally at ease while Spencer was embracing me as Mayon was when Panganoron did. It was terrible that I met Spencer late and that I failed to express the love I have for him.

I was looking for a reason to live, then I found him, he found me***but I never thought that the reason that I wanted to live would also be the reason why I wanted to die.

"I wish he was here." I whispered.

I felt the wind kiss my cheeks.

"See you soon, Spencer."

Chapter 10

DOC AUGUST POV

DAYS AGO......

"SPENCER." I called, he was laying in his bed, Spencer is my best friend since 8th grade

"Hey, Doc." he muttered and laugh a bit

"Paris, is—"

"Don't let her, please."

Tears started to form in his eyes as he pressed his lips together.

"I love her, and I couldn't let her donate her heart so I could live, because I would kill myself if she die."

"So how do I tell her that you don't want her to donate her heart, pretty sure she would insist?" I ask

"Tell her that she has some sort of sickness, Doc." he replied as he closed his eyes.

Paris took the test so I examined it. She has cancer, an incurable one, she doesn't experience some symptoms, so I should give it a second look to more doctors out there.

"Code Blue in room 1214." the nurse shouted, Spencer's room. I immediately ran there and based on Spencer's face, I checked his pulse, he was no longer here, I left the room, Paris was in there, I lost my one and only best friend.

I closed my office door, as I sitted down on my swivel chair, I looked at the frame as my tears started flowing.

"Sp-Spencer." I stifle.

I covered my face with my palm as I let it out. "I never thought losing you was this heart breaking, Goodbye, my dear friend." I washed my face before going out, going back to my friend. I gave Paris the ring and the letter, Spencer asked me to do it, but when she stood off, there's blood, plenty of it.

"PA-Paris."

She was pregnant with Spencer's child. Not only does she lose Spencer but she also loses her angel. Where in Paris now, Paris and Spencer are getting married in the church where we can see the Eiffel tower.

Mrs. Prescott held Paris's urn and Mr. Martin held Spencer's urn.

"Now, I pronounce you husband and wife." The priest said tearing up, everyone wears white to this day, their wedding and the day we will spread their ashes in the Eiffel tower.

The City of France, Paris was the city of love, and Paris, the girl who caught Spencer's heart was our city of love.

Days after Spencer died, it was confirmed that Paris was diagnosed with cancer, a few months after, she followed Spencer in the after life

They had a tough journey together, but both of them survived it. They both don't want to lose each other but destiny made its own way to separate them apart and destiny was the one who brought them back together.

They might not be here now, but I know Paris Maverick Martin and Spencer Thaddeus Martin with their little angel are living the family life in the afterlife.

I knew Spencer wanted to hear the 3 words from Paris, and Paris finally said it when Spencer was long gone.

"Congrats, Mr and Mrs. Martin, may you have the best in the afterlife."

About the Author

Akisss Mora

Akisss Mora was a secret person, a student, a person who is fond of writing sad novels and poetries. He kept his stories and poems to herself, never sharing them with anyone. She wrote about the darkness that haunted her, the sorrow that consumed her, and the pain that kept her awake at night. Despite the sadness in her writing, she found a cathartic release in it, a way to express the emotions that she didn't know how to process.

www.ingramcontent.com/pod-product-compliance
Lightning Source LLC
LaVergne TN
LVHW041553070526
838199LV00046B/1951